Silly Sausage
and
the Spooks

by Michaela Morgan
illustrated by Dee Shulman

PICTURE WINDOW BOOKS
Minneapolis, Minnesota

Editors: Jacqueline Wolfe, Christianne Jones
Page Production: Brandie E. Shoemaker
Creative Director: Keith Griffin
Editorial Director: Carol Jones

First American edition published in 2007 by
Picture Window Books
5115 Excelsior Boulevard
Suite 232
Minneapolis, MN 55416
877-845-8392
www.picturewindowbooks.com

First published in 2001 by
A&C Black Publishers Limited
38 Soho Square
London W1D 3HB

Text copyright © Michaela Morgan 2001
Illustrations copyright © Dee Shulman 2001

Printed in the United States of America.

Library of Congress Cataloging-in-Publication Data
Morgan, Michaela.
Silly Sausage and the spooks / by Michaela Morgan & Dee Shulman. — 1st
American ed.
p. cm. — (Read-it! chapter books)
Summary: When the cats, Fitz and Spatz, call Sausage the dog a coward and tease
him into spending the night in a haunted house, they are in for a fright of their own.
ISBN-13: 978-1-4048-2736-3 (hardcover)
ISBN-10: 1-4048-2736-6 (hardcover)
[1. Fear—Fiction. 2. Haunted houses—Fiction. 3. Dachshunds—Fiction.
4. Dogs—Fiction. 5. Cats—Fiction.] I. Shulman, Dee, ill. II. Title. III. Series.

PZ7.M8255Sils 2006
[E]—dc22   2006003437

Table of Contents

Chapter One

There are all sorts of dogs in the world. Big dogs, little dogs, fat dogs, and skinny dogs.

One special dog is very long, very low, and is as plump as a sausage.

Sausage! That's me!

Sausage lives in a house with Elly and Jack,

Gran,

and Fitz and Spatz, the family cats.

I'm Fitz.

I'm Spatz.

Fitz is a smart cat, but he's also a very sneaky, snooty cat.

He loves to laugh at Sausage. He loves to look down on Sausage. He loves to steal Sausage's bed.

9

Spatz is a big cat. He's a burly cat.
He's a bit of a bully. He loves to
bully Sausage.

SLURP

CHOMP

SAUSAGE

He loves to steal Sausage's food.

Chapter Two

Fitz and Spatz play tricks on
other animals.

swing!

stomp!

They love to play tricks on Sausage.

They both like to make fun of Sausage.

They tease him.

They call him names.

They both like to frighten him.

BOO!!!!

HA!

HA!

"I wasn't really scared," Sausage protested. "I'm big and brave."

I've done some very brave things in my time, you know.

The cats just sneered and snickered.

"Not scared?" Spatz sneered.

"Big and brave?" Fitz snickered.

"Well, prove it!" they said.

Spatz and Fitz started to plot
and plan.

They whispered.

They giggled.

They snickered.

Then they said, "All you have to do
to prove you are brave is one thing."

Chapter Three

Sausage ate an extra-large dinner of sizzling sausages to prepare himself.

He practiced his scariest looks.

He practiced his loudest barks.

Then it was time to go.

The haunted house had been empty for a long time. It was old, crumbly, big, dusty, and full of cobwebs. Nobody ever went near it. Nobody ever wanted to go in. Sausage wasn't sure he wanted to go in, either.

"In you go, Silly Sausage," said the cats. "We'll keep guard to make sure you stay in there all night."

Sausage went in. The floor was thick with dust. Everything was quiet. The darkness grew, and so did the shadows. Sausage began to shiver.

Four glowing eyes glared at him.
They belonged to the cats.

"We'll really give that silly Sausage
something to shiver about. We'll make
spooky sounds," the cats said.

"We'll make spooky shapes," Fitz said.

"We'll dress up as ghosts," Spatz said.

"We'll give that silly dog the fright of his life," they both said.

Be afraid!

Be very afraid!

Chapter Four

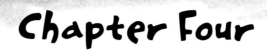

Fitz began creeping around.
Spatz began sneaking around.
The floors creaked.

Sausage began to shake.

Spatz started whispering.

Fitz started hissing.

They found an old
chain and rattled it.

Sausage began to
shiver and shake.

Spatz made a spooky howling noise.
Fitz joined in.

Sausage put his paws over his eyes.
He lay there shaking and listening
to all the wailing, howling, creaking,
and squeaking around him.

"What can I do? What can I do?"
he worried.

Then he had an idea.

"I will close my eyes and think of something cheerful—like sausages," he decided. And that's just what he did.

Soon Sausage felt warm, happy, and safe. He drifted off into a dreamy sleep.

Chapter Five

Meanwhile, the cats were still plotting.

I've got a brilliant idea!

Wicked!

"We'll put these white sheets over us and hide at the top of the stairs. Then we can flap and screech and whoop and swoop down on Sausage. That will really spook him," Fitz said.

"That will show how scared he is,"
Spatz said. "That will make him
shake like jelly. Jelly and Sausage."

The cats crept up the stairs and got
their sheets.

"Did you hear something?"
asked Fitz.

Suddenly, there was an eerie
sound coming from above.
The cats shivered.

OOOOOOOOOOO

"Did you see something?"
whispered Spatz.

High, high above them
something was moving.
Its eyes were glowing.
It was white.

It was flapping. It
swooped and flapped
at them. It screeched!

Chapter Six

Sausage was still asleep, dreaming of sausages. In his dream, a pan of sausages was sizzling. Then, with a loud noise they exploded. Aaaggh!

Sausage jumped up and barked.

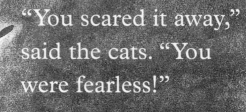

The *thing* flapped away.

"You scared it away," said the cats. "You were fearless!"

Sausage opened his eyes. "What is it?" he asked.

He took a closer look and said, "Oh, it's a bird."

I like birds. Nice birdie.

The owl hooted softly.

Whooooooooo.

"I've never heard of CATS being afraid of birds!" said Sausage.

"We weren't really scared," they said, but Sausage knew the truth.

"Everyone's scared sometimes," he said.

The cats crept home, embarrassed
and ashamed.

Sausage trotted home with his head held high. Nobody could call him a scaredy-cat!

Look for More *Read-it!* Chapter Books

Looking for a specific title? A complete list
of *Read-it!* Chapter Books is available on our Web site:
www.picturewindowbooks.com